PEANUTS®

SNOOPY
Came to Play

Ready-to-Read

By Charles M. Schulz
Adapted by Tina Gallo
Illustrated by Vicki Sc

SIMON SPOTLIGHT
New York   London   Toronto   Sydney   New Delhi

Here is a list of all the words you will find in this book. Sound them out before you begin reading the story.

Names:

 Snoopy

 Woodstock

SIMON SPOTLIGHT
An imprint of Simon & Schuster Children's Publishing Division
1230 Avenue of the Americas, New York, New York 10020
This Simon Spotlight edition June 2018
© 2018 Peanuts Worldwide LLC
SIMON SPOTLIGHT, READY-TO-READ, and colophon are registered trademarks of Simon & Schuster, Inc.
For information about special discounts for bulk purchases, please contact
Simon & Schuster Special Sales at 1-866-506-1949 or business@simonandschuster.com.
Manufactured in the United States of America 0518 LAK
2 4 6 8 10 9 7 5 3 1
ISBN 978-1-5344-1507-2 (hc) ISBN 978-1-5344-1506-5 (pbk) ISBN 978-1-5344-1508-9 (eBook)

Word families:

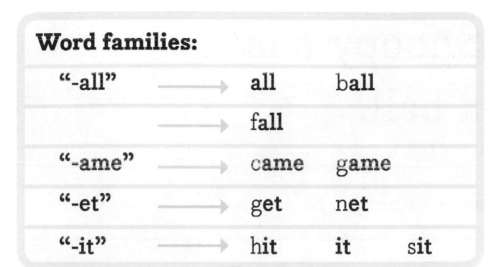

"-all"	→	all	ball
	→	fall	
"-ame"	→	came	game
"-et"	→	get	net
"-it"	→	hit	it	sit

Sight words:

a	and	can	day	has
not	play	the	to	too
will	with			

Bonus words:

| again | racket | |

Ready to go? Happy reading!

Don't miss the questions about the story
on the last page of this book.

Snoopy has
a ball.

Snoopy has
a racket.

Snoopy came
to play.

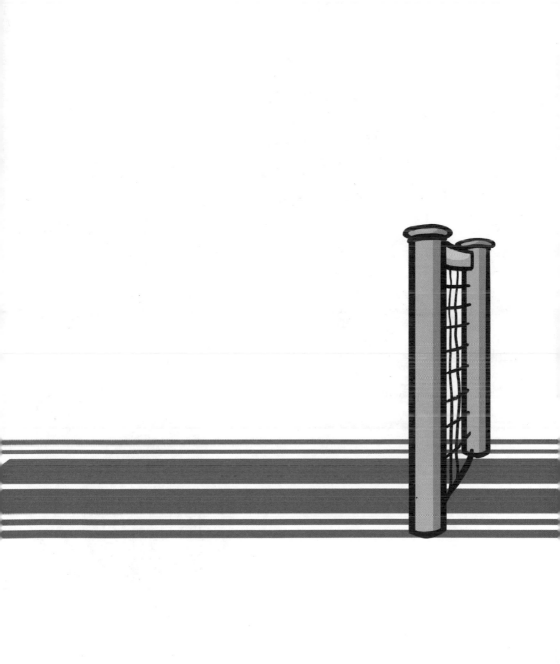

Woodstock came
to play too.

Snoopy can hit the ball.

The ball can hit Snoopy.

Can Woodstock hit the ball?

Woodstock can hit the ball!

Snoopy can hit the net!

Snoopy will
get a ball.

Snoopy can
hit the ball.

The ball can hit the net.

Snoopy can hit the ball again.

Will the ball fall?

The ball will fall.
Will Snoopy get it?

Snoopy will not
get the ball.

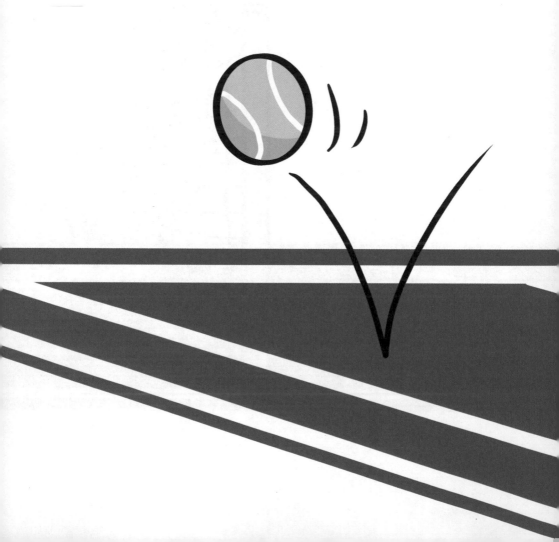

Woodstock will sit
with Snoopy.

Woodstock and Snoopy
will play a game.

Snoopy and Woodstock
will play all day.

Now that you have read the story, can you answer these questions?

1. What does Snoopy bring with him to play a game of tennis?

2. Is Snoopy happy or sad at the end of the story?

3. In this story, you read the rhyming words "get" and "net." Can you think of other words that rhyme with "get" and "net"?

Great job!
You are a reading star!